THE
CARLTON
TREASURE

THE CARLTON TREASURE

AND OTHER MYSTERY STORIES
Compiled by the Editors
of
Highlights for Children

CONTENTS

THE CARLTON TREASURE

By L. H. Phinney

The farmhouse Ted Grant lived in had been built long ago, no one knew how long. It had belonged to the Grant family for generations. An uncle, Abel Grant, had lived in it alone for years. Then, when Ted was ten, he and his father and mother had moved to the old farm—and learned of its mystery.

It began with a note they found in a box of old letters that had belonged to Uncle Abel. Mrs. Grant was clearing out the attic when she found the box. The letters were old and yellow, of no special interest save for their stamps. This note had no stamp, and part of it had been torn away or eaten by mice. What was left read:

I have lived for years on the Carlton treasure. If there is any left when I am gone, whoever finds it may have it. It is in this house. The key is in the old clock.

Abel Grant

"What is this Carlton treasure?" Mrs. Grant asked.

"One of my ancestors was captain of a ship called the *Carlton* back in the 1790s," Mr. Grant replied. "But I don't recall anything about a treasure. And Abel never mentioned it. But he was much older than I—a silent, secret man."

The grocer added to the mystery a few days later. "Hear you're living on the old Grant farm," he said. "You're Abel's brother? I wonder if he left you any of the old coins he used to have. He used to pay for groceries with 'em. Foreign—Spanish, English, Italian. Most of 'em were gold. Hard to figure what they were worth, sometimes. I sold most of 'em in the city. I told Abel they could be sold but he wouldn't bother. Better look the old house over and see if you can find any more."

Mr. Grant looked the house over and found nothing except a small brass key hanging inside the old kitchen clock. But where was the lock it fitted?

Ted also looked the house over, from cellar to attic. And one day he found something. It was in a closet at the head of the stairs. He saw something shine in the light of his flashlight, in a crack in the floor. He took his jackknife and dug it out.

It was an old Spanish coin dated 1780. It looked as if it had been dropped edge-first into the crack in the floor, then stepped on and driven almost out of sight.

After that, the whole family hunted. But nothing more was found. Ted kept on looking, though. On rainy days when he couldn't go out, he would take his flashlight and hunt for the treasure.

He was hunting today. It was raining hard out-side. Naturally, he looked again in the closet where he had found the gold coin. The cracks in the floor yielded nothing. He had looked there a hundred times, anyway.

The closet walls were now covered with hanging clothes. Ted swung them aside and examined the cracks in the wallboards. In doing so, he accidentally hit the back wall with his flashlight. It sounded hollow! He pushed the wall with his hand. It wasn't solid. It gave a little.

9

The boards were uneven. There seemed to be a panel like a door, about three feet high, where the boards sunk lower than the others. But there was no keyhole. There was nothing to show that it really was a door, but it looked like one.

Ted thought it must be a door. He felt all around the wall, close to the edge of the panel. Suddenly, his fingers struck something. It felt like a knot in the wood. He turned the flashlight on it. It was a knot, and it seemed to be loose, but it wouldn't pull out. He pressed it—and the panel rattled. He pressed the knot and pushed the panel again. But nothing happened this time.

Then Ted saw a knothole in the panel, close to one edge. He put his finger in it and pulled as he pressed the loose knot again. The panel slid a little to one side, then to its full width, leaving an opening about two feet wide. Only darkness lay beyond it.

Ted turned the beam of the flashlight into the darkness. There seemed to be a small room beyond, maybe six feet square. It smelled airless and musty. Cautiously, Ted entered the little room—but first he blocked the door open with a shoe.

The floor of the room was covered with dust. One wall was brick—the large old chimney, they learned later. The other walls were rough boards. In one corner of the room stood a small old-fashioned table. On it was an iron box with a heavy handle.

Ted could hardly lift the box. But he managed to stagger with it out of the little room and down the stairs, shouting, "I've found the Carlton treasure!"

With a bang, he set the box on the kitchen table in front of his startled parents. They opened it with the old brass key. Inside was half a box of old gold coins and a piece of parchment. The note read:

Salvaged from a wreck off Galleon Reef, March 3, 1794, on my last trip as Captain of the Carlton. *Theodore P. Grant*

"Look!" said Ted. "His name was the same as mine. We both found the same treasure!"

"The Carlton treasure has served us well," said Ted's father, "first Captain Theodore, then Uncle Abel. And, unless I miss my guess, those coins are worth enough to let a sea captain of long ago help put his namesake through college."

Island Mystery

By Christine M. Ianson

"Are you still awake, Libby?" Sarah sat up in her sleeping bag to ask her sister.

Libby said, "I keep thinking about Caccio."

Sarah and Libby listened to the waves slapping against the huge boulders around Indian Island. Their tent was pitched high on a hill. Through the screen triangle on the side of the tent, they saw the stars sprinkled like tiny diamonds on an ink-blue sky. A gentle breeze brought in the scent of dried pine needles mingled with campfire smoke. The girls were tired, but they couldn't fall asleep. Who *was* Caccio?

It had been an exciting day. Sarah had convinced her father that she and Libby were old enough for an overnight stay on the island. "We are both good swimmers," Sarah had said to her father. "We know how to set up the pup tent, and we'll catch fish for supper."

The girls packed their gear into the rowboat. "Good-bye," they said as they rowed away.

"You're on your own," called their father. "Be careful and have fun!"

Sarah swelled with pride. She felt grown up. This was the first time she was totally responsible for herself and her younger sister. As she dipped her oar into the clear water she said, "Look at the rocks on the bottom, Libby. Guess how deep they are."

"About three feet, I bet," Libby answered.

"That's what you think," said Sarah. "Take our anchor and throw it overboard."

Libby plunged the anchor into the water. Almost all twenty feet of rope uncoiled before the anchor reached bottom. She pulled the anchor up again. "Wow," said Libby. "Is that deep!"

She was just a bit uneasy as she watched the rocks disappear while the water got deeper and deeper. She was glad they were wearing life jackets.

As Sarah rowed, the boat rocked gently in the waves. Libby looked up at the surrounding mountains. They formed a green crown around the lake. She enjoyed the warm sun on her back and forgot all about the depth of the water. Soon Libby and Sarah pulled their rowboat onto a flat rock in shallow water at Indian Island. Libby tied the rope to a nearby tree.

First the girls unpacked their tent and fishing gear. Then they searched for a good campsite. By the time they spread their sleeping bags over the soft pine boughs in their pup tent, they were hungry.

Libby said, "Let's take a break and have a snack." She brought out the paper bag of brownies their mother had packed for them.

After they had eaten some, Sarah said, "Don't take these brownies into our tent, Libby, unless you want a raccoon to share your sleeping bag." Libby put the food into their orange knapsack and hung it on a branch.

"We ought to start fishing if we want supper tonight," said Sarah. With their poles over their shoulders, the girls walked barefoot across the island. They found a ledge where they could see fish swimming under a boulder. The fishing went well. Libby caught a good-sized bass, and Sarah reeled in a ten-inch rainbow trout.

It was almost dark. The girls were carrying their catch back to camp. Suddenly, Libby called, "Hey, Sarah, take a look at this!" On a rough area on the side of a smooth boulder, Libby had just scraped her big toe. That's how she discovered the tombstone. "I'm not sure, but I think I'm standing on a grave," she said reverently.

"I'll bet you are," Sarah said impatiently. "Come on. You have to build the fire, and I have to clean these fish."

"Sarah, there really is something here!"

"OK, but you'd better not be fooling." *It was probably left as a joke by some other campers*, Sarah thought to herself.

Libby was bending over the rock. "It looks like a tombstone chiseled right into this granite."

Sarah looked. Hewn into the solid rock was the shape of a shield with the name CACCIO inscribed at the top. Under it the girls could barely read:

BORN MAY 2, 1893
DIED MAY 6, 1908

"Today is May sixth," said Libby. "Somebody died on Indian Island on this date in 1908."

Sarah said, "If you take the difference between the dates 1908 and 1893, you get fifteen. That means that Caccio was fifteen years old when she died. That's only four years older than I am and five years older than you, Libby."

There were three more lines. Some of the letters were blurred by weathering. Slowly and carefully, Sarah traced them with her finger:

She was only a —— ——
but very l——l to
F A D U R

It was all they could make out.

When they got back to their camp, the girls made a fire, fried their fish for supper, and went to bed in their tent. Exhausted from the day's events, they should have been fast asleep by now. But the girls lay awake, puzzling over the mystery of this fifteen-year-old girl who had died here so long ago.

"Could it have been an Indian maiden?" asked Libby. "No," answered Sarah, "she died in 1908. The Indians must have been gone from here long before that."

Whoever took the trouble to carve the tombstone must have loved Caccio very much, Libby thought. Why was she buried here all alone on this tiny island?

"Do you think there was a funeral?" Libby asked her sister.

"I don't know," said Sarah. She thought for a long time. Then she remembered the leaf rubbings she did in her science class. Sarah jumped up and said, "I know how we can learn the secret of the tombstone. Now let's get some sleep."

The girls were up at sunrise. Low-hanging clouds formed misty curtains in front of the mountains. The pale sun formed a silver path on the surface of the lake. Sarah stirred the ashes of last night's campfire. She found a firm piece of charcoal. Then she asked Libby to get the paper bag with the brownies. She carefully ripped it open at the folds and made a flat piece of brown paper.

At the grave marker, Sarah asked Libby to cover the engraved letters with the paper. "It's very important that you don't let it slip," she said. Sarah took the piece of charcoal she had brought along and began to rub it all over the brown paper that Libby was holding up for her.

"I get it," said Libby. "By rubbing the paper, we'll get an impression of the missing letters."

Sure enough, when Sarah had finished, all the letters on the engraved tombstone were clear on the paper. Libby grinned at Sarah as she read:

CACCIO
BORN MAY 2, 1893
DIED MAY 6, 1908
She was only a pug dog
but very loyal to
FADUR

Caccio was a pug-dog! Her master was Fadur, and he must have loved her. The girls walked back to their tent in silence. They thought of Caccio and Fadur, and of the secret they had learned.

Inspector Hector

By Elaine Pageler

Only yesterday I handed out my "Inspector Hector, Detective for Hire" cards to the kids at school. Today someone called me up and offered me a missing-person case.

"Come quick, Inspector Hector!" said the voice on the telephone. "This is Jennifer, and I need you. My Grandma Rose is missing!"

I grabbed the bag that holds all my detective gear and raced over to Jennifer's house. She was waiting on the front step.

"Tell me all about the missing person," I said. "When did you discover that your Grandma Rose was gone?"

Jennifer gave me a surprised look. "Not my Grandma Rose! It's my grandma's *rose* that's missing."

My smile disappeared. "You mean like a flower or a bush?" I demanded.

Jennifer nodded. "Grandma asked me to care for the rose while she went on a trip. It was sitting here in a pot when I went to the beach yesterday. When I came back today, it was gone."

I was disappointed. A missing person was more exciting than a missing flower. But a plant case is better than no case at all. I pulled a pair of binoculars out of my bag and scanned the neighborhood.

"There's a rose planted in your neighbor's front yard," I told her.

Jennifer's eyes widened in surprise. "There was no rose in his yard yesterday," she said.

"Definitely suspicious," I said, dashing over to the neighbor's house. Jennifer was calling something after me, but I didn't stop. A rule in my detective's handbook says to follow up every lead quickly.

The name *Smith* was on the door knocker. When the man answered the door, I flashed him a smile and said, "Hello, Mr. Smith. That's a beautiful rose you have. Where did you get it?"

Mr. Smith beamed. "I bought it yesterday during the big sale at Long's Nursery."

"May I take a picture of you and your rose?" I asked as I pulled my instant camera out of my bag.

The minute the picture developed, I dashed down to Long's Nursery. Jennifer ran after me. "Wait a minute," she called.

I didn't stop. Another rule in my handbook says to let nothing interfere with your investigation. I showed the picture to the store manager and asked, "Did this man buy this rose from you yesterday?"

"Sorry, kid," the manager answered. "There were so many people at our sale yesterday that I wouldn't remember my own mother. But the rose looks like it could be one of ours."

"It is," panted Jennifer. "I was trying to tell Hector that Mr. Smith's rose is too healthy to be Grandma's. Hers looked sort of dry and yellow."

"It probably needs fertilizing," the man said. "I bet the leaves were dropping off, too."

Jennifer nodded. "They were."

Another rule in my handbook says to always adjust your thinking when one lead doesn't solve the case. I adjusted fast. "Let's look for a trail of leaves! Come on, Jennifer!" I shouted, grabbing my magnifying glass out of my detective bag and sprinting back to her house.

Sure enough, there was a trail of small, curled-up leaves going down her steps and out to the curb. But that's where the trail stopped. "The thief must have put the rose in a car," I said.

Jennifer nodded. "Another dead end," she said, shaking her head.

Just then I spotted a pool of oil on the street. "No!" I yelled. "Not a dead end. Lucky for us, your thief has a big oil leak in his car. We just have to follow that black line."

We were hot on the trail. Five blocks later, the oil leak led into a driveway. A grease-covered man stood beside a jacked-up van, and a yellowish rose sat on a bench nearby.

Jennifer started to open her mouth, but I didn't wait to hear what she had to say. According to my handbook, this was the time to get the police. I was on my way to find the closest telephone when I heard Jennifer's voice.

"Hi, Bert," she said smiling. "We're looking for my grandma's rose."

"Yes, I suppose you would be, Jennifer," answered the man. "When I mowed your lawn yesterday, your plant looked sick, so I brought it home to fertilize it. Then my van broke down."

I skidded to a stop. Obviously, this guy with the leaky van was the family's gardener.

Jennifer smiled when she saw me returning. "You solved the case, Inspector Hector! You found my grandma's rose! Would you help me carry it home?"

My handbook didn't say anything about carrying things for people. But the TV detectives are always nice to clients, so it must be all right. Furthermore, we had to discuss my finder's fee.

When we got back to Jennifer's house, I found out her grandma had bought a new rose. "That's OK," said Jennifer. "I'll give this one to Inspector Hector for his fee."

I picked up the old rose and tried not to look disappointed. TV detectives make money, but I couldn't even pay for the film in my camera.

When I was halfway down the block, Jennifer called my name. This time I stopped, since there was no hot lead to follow. It's lucky I did, because she said, "Mr. Smith wants to buy that picture of himself and his rose. Will you sell it to him?"

I sold the picture. So I had solved my first case and made some money, too. Everything had gone well, although my handbook needed one new rule. I went home and wrote in a rule about always listening to my clients. Listening might make my next assignment a little easier.

KEY
to the
FAIR

By Linda Rogers

Michael bounded into the house, carrying the newspaper. He snapped the rubber band off, wrapped it around the front doorknob, and then plopped down onto the sofa.

"Well, what exciting mystery are you reading today, sleuth?" he asked with a chuckle.

Lisa put her book down and looked over at her older brother.

"You're sure friendly," she said.

"Maybe it's my new job," he replied. "Mr. Chun hired me to work in his fish market while he's out of town this weekend." Michael held up a key on a large rubber band and waved it proudly in the air. "I'll work tomorrow afternoon. Then I'll open the store Saturday and work all day."

"What's he going to pay you?" Lisa asked.

"Twenty dollars," Michael answered.

"Twenty dollars!"

"That's right. By the way, what are you going to do for money? You know, the street fair is next week. And you don't have enough money to buy even a box of popcorn."

"How do you know?" Lisa demanded. "Have you been peeking in my piggy bank?"

"Are you kidding? I couldn't get into your room without a bulldozer! That place is a jungle."

"It suits me just fine," she answered. "I know where everything is."

"Of course you do," Michael teased. "Everything is on the floor."

"Just because you file your toothbrush under T . . ."

"I do not!" Michael laughed as he got up and headed for the kitchen. Lisa followed.

"Going to have a peanut butter and banana sandwich and half a glass of chocolate milk?"

"How did you know?" Michael looked puzzled.

Lisa laughed. "Because you're so predictable. I always know what you're going to do."

"What do you mean?" Michael opened the peanut butter jar.

"I mean that tomorrow morning you'll get up and put on your blue corduroy pants and your red-striped T-shirt. That's what you always wear on Friday." Michael looked surprised. "Then you'll come down to breakfast," she went on. "You'll toast two pieces of bread. You'll put butter on the first and honey on the second. Then you'll sit at the table and eat them—the buttered one first. Then . . ."

"Lisa, you have the brain of a cheap detective! You've been reading too many mysteries. Did you ever think that maybe there's such a thing as being too observant?"

"And maybe there's such a thing as being too organized," she responded.

"Never," Michael said. He bit into his peanut butter and banana sandwich.

When Michael came home from the fish market the next day, he was wearing blue cords and a red-striped T-shirt. He walked in the front door with the newspaper in his hand. He wrapped the rubber band around the doorknob and plopped down onto the sofa. Lisa watched him.

"How's the fish business?" she asked.

"It stinks," he laughed. "But at least I'll enjoy myself at the fair," he said, reaching into his pockets.

"Who's going to pay your way?" He lifted a vase of flowers on the coffee table and looked under it.

"What are you looking for," Lisa asked.

"Nothing," he snapped.

"Well, you don't have to get angry."

"I'm not angry. I just can't seem to find it."

"Find what," she asked.

"The Chun key."

"The chunky what?" Lisa asked calmly.

"The Chun key!" Michael bellowed. "The key to Mr. Chun's fish market!"

"You lost the key to the fish market?"

"I didn't lose it. I just can't find it." Michael was getting more upset.

"Well, stay cool, Michael. Just try to organize your thoughts. Where did you last see it?"

"I know I had it when I left the market because I locked the door behind me," he insisted.

"Then what did you do?"

"Oh, Lisa, stop all the detective stuff. I've got to go back to the market!" He headed for the door.

"Wait a minute." Lisa grabbed his arm and pulled him into the kitchen. "We might need this." She picked up a flashlight from on top of the refrigerator and they both ran out the door.

On the way to the fish market, Lisa asked again, "What did you do after you locked the door?"

"I took some garbage to the bin in the alley. That's the first place to look."

They were out of breath when they reached the alley. Lisa shined the flashlight into the dark bin and groaned.

"Fishheads and bones! Oh, Michael, I don't know if I can do this."

She held the flashlight with one hand and her nose with the other as Michael rummaged around the garbage bin. But it was no use. There was no key to be found.

A thorough search of the area turned up nothing. And the only things they found on the route home were two pennies, a bottle cap, and dozens of gum wrappers.

Reaching the house exhausted, Michael threw himself into a chair. He picked up the newspaper, snapped off the rubber band, and opened to the sports page. Lisa's mouth dropped open, and she glanced over at the front door.

"Michael," she cooed, "how badly do you want that key?"

"How badly? I want it very badly and you know it! Do you mean to say that you know . . ."

"I mean, what is it worth to you, Michael? I could use some money for the fair. Five dollars would be nice."

"Five dollars! That's robbery!"

"OK, never mind." She got up to leave.

"Wait! OK, you get the five dollars, you thief! Now, where is the key? How did you find it?"

"Observation, my dear brother, observation."

"Well, get on with it, will you?" Michael was growing impatient.

"When you first came in this afternoon, you had a newspaper in your hand, as you always do. You walked through the door and wrapped the rubber band around the doorknob, just as you always do. But just now you picked up that same newspaper and took a rubber band off it." Lisa smiled a satisfied smile. But Michael was just confused.

"So what?" he asked.

"So," she continued, "if the rubber band was still on the newspaper here, what did you wrap around the doorknob when you came in earlier?"

Michael sprang to his feet and ran to the door. Sure enough, hanging from the doorknob on a rubber band was the key Mr. Chun had given him.

"Lisa, you're a genius! A real genius! I'll never make fun of your detective brain again."

Lisa smiled but said nothing as she sat down, picked up her mystery book, and began reading.

The Orchid Mystery

By June Swanson

As Erin held up the measuring cup to check the level of water, she noticed a slight movement reflected in its glass side. Turning around, she saw a figure bending over a desk at the other end of the classroom. Even from the back, she recognized Audrey Manchester.

"Audrey," she called, "what are you doing here? No one is supposed to be in the science room after school. I had special permission to do some work on my bean-plant experiment."

"I . . . I forgot something," stammered Audrey. She walked nervously toward Erin. Her footsteps echoed in the quiet room.

Erin continued working in silence. She didn't know Audrey very well. None of the kids did. Erin couldn't even think of anything to say to her.

Audrey gestured timidly around the room. "Mrs. Brennen sure has a lot of plants, doesn't she?"

As Erin nodded, her short, blond hair bobbed up and down. "She loves them. And some are very valuable, like that yellow orchid over there."

Audrey bent over the orchid.

Erin checked her experiment chart. "Well, I'm finished. I'll see you tomorrow."

The next morning Erin hurried into science class just as the bell rang. A noisy group was clustered around Mrs. Brennen's desk.

"What's the matter?" Erin asked.

Excited voices answered. "The orchid plant is gone! Someone stole it!"

Mrs. Brennen seemed relieved to see Erin. "I've been waiting for you. You were in here after school yesterday. Do you remember if the orchid was here then?"

"Yes, it was. We even talked about it."

"We?"

"Audrey was here, too. She forgot something."

Mrs. Brennen frowned. "Well, I'll ask the custodians later. Maybe one of them knows something about it. Let's get to work now."

As Erin walked down the aisle, she saw Audrey hunched over her desk, intently reading a book. Audrey's fingers nervously bent the corners of the pages up and down.

This little action started gears turning in Erin's head. Audrey had seemed nervous yesterday after school, too. "Oh, no," thought Erin. "Audrey stole the orchid! And I'm the one who told her how valuable it was. I should have known she couldn't be trusted!"

Erin had a hard time concentrating the rest of the day. All she could think about was the orchid.

As the last bell rang, Erin hurried out the front door. After looking around carefully, she slipped behind a tall evergreen bush. She didn't wait long.

In a few minutes Audrey ran out the door, raced down the block, and turned the corner. Erin followed. Audrey slowed to a fast walk. Erin slowed, too. Audrey didn't seem to know she was being followed, and Erin tried to keep it that way.

As Audrey headed toward the railroad tracks, the houses became smaller and shabbier. Suddenly, she turned into the path to an old, weatherbeaten house. Audrey hurried to the front door, knocked twice, and let herself in with a key.

Erin stopped. If only there were some trees or bushes to hide behind, she could get closer to the house without being seen. She felt certain this small house held the answer to the orchid mystery. Was this the hideout of a gang of thieves? Maybe it was a place where people could sell things they had stolen. Erin wasn't sure.

Bending over to make herself as small as possible, Erin tiptoed to the side of the house and silently slid along the wall. She could hear Audrey talking inside, but the voice that answered was weak and muffled. Erin couldn't make out the words.

Now Erin was at the back corner of the house. She peered around cautiously. Nothing. She continued along the back of the house until she spotted a small window. If only she could see inside, maybe she could find out what was going on. Erin slowly raised her head, until her eyes were just above the windowsill.

Audrey sat with her back to the window. Erin raised herself higher. She could see a bed and a figure lying on it.

Next to the bed was a table piled high with old newspapers and magazines. And on top of the messy pile sat the yellow orchid!

Erin slid to the ground. "I was right," she muttered. "Audrey *did* take the orchid! Now what do I do?"

Her thoughts were interrupted by the sound of a chair sliding on the bare floor inside. She could hear Audrey's footsteps crossing the floor. Erin made her way back to the corner of the house and along the side wall. A door slammed. Audrey was walking down the path toward the street.

Before Erin realized it, she had called, "Audrey!"

The girl spun around, startled. Erin walked right up to her. At the sight of Erin, Audrey's mouth flew open. "What are you doing here?"

"I followed you from school. I thought maybe you knew something about the orchid, and I wanted to find out. You did take it, didn't you?"

Audrey's face turned white. "I . . . I didn't really steal it. I've never stolen anything. I just wanted to borrow it for a few days. My grandmother is very sick, and I didn't have money to buy her flowers or anything. I needed *something* to cheer her up. With all those plants, I didn't think Mrs. Brennen would miss just one."

Erin was stunned. Her anger was slowly turning to sympathy. Audrey just looked down at the ground, frowning. Finally, Erin broke the heavy silence. "You should have asked Mrs. Brennen. I'm sure she would have let you borrow a plant. I know where she lives. Why don't we go and talk to her right now? She'll be happy to know the orchid is safe."

Seeing the frightened look on Audrey's face, Erin continued. "It'll be all right. Honest. She'll understand. I'll help you explain it."

Audrey looked surprised. "You'll help *me?*"

"Sure." Erin smiled. "That's what friends are for. Come on. Let's go!"

The Case of the
Flyaway Parakeet

by Stephanie Moody

The Canine Detective Agency was just opening for business when its owners heard a strange
noise. It sounded like someone was crying.

"Oh, no. Oh, no," the sobbing voice said. It was
coming from inside the apartment building where
the three detectives lived.

"Quick," said Tommy, "someone is in trouble.
We must help."

"Follow me," said Sam. "My dog Brutus will
find the noise with his sharp hearing."

Sam and Brutus bounded up the front stairs. Brutus was so big he leaped the stairs three at a time. He was at the top, racing into the building.

Marcus and his dog Tracker followed. Tracker was so big he bounded up the stairs two at a time. *Plop, plop, plop.* He was at the top.

Tommy looked at his dog Lucky. Lucky was barely big enough to climb the stairs. Most of the time Lucky needed a boost. To save time, Tommy scooped Lucky into his arms. They were in a hurry.

Once inside the building, Brutus led them straight to the strange crying sound.

Sam pounded on the door. "We are the Canine Detective Agency. Let us in," he said.

The door didn't open.

Marcus banged on the door. *Whack, whack, whack.* "We have come to help you."

Nothing happened.

"Maybe the door is stuck," said Sam to Marcus. "Let's both push together. On the count of three. Ready. One . . . two . . . three."

The door swung open. The boys and the dogs crashed through the opening, *kaPLOP*, landing in a heap on the floor.

"Don't mind my friends," said Tommy, who had just reached the doorway. "They were in a hurry to help you. Now, why were you crying?"

"M-m-my name is Jason Kline," said a boy, wiping his tears. "I've been taking care of my aunt's parakeet while she is away. Her name is Hoppity. She likes to hop a lot."

"Your aunt likes to hop?"

"No, her bird. And while I was feeding her . . ."

"You have to feed your aunt?"

"No, *no*. Listen," said Jason. "My aunt's *parakeet* hopped out of her cage and flew out the window. Now I'll never find her."

"This is not a case for us," said Marcus, who had finally gotten untangled from Brutus and Sam and Tracker. "Even Tracker can't follow the scent of a flying bird."

"And Brutus can't catch a flying bird, either," said Sam. "We cannot help you at all."

"Not so fast," said Tommy, looking around the room. "Something strange is going on here, something very strange."

"What is so strange about a bird flying out of a window?" asked Sam.

"Nothing," said Tommy, "if the window is open."

Everybody looked at the closed window. Then they looked at Jason.

"Well, I didn't really *see* her fly out the window," he said. "But if she didn't, then . . ."

"Then what?" asked Tommy.

Jason pointed at Pepper, the cat. "Then Pepper must have gobbled her up. I had my back turned for only a second."

"And that's when Pepper swallowed Hoppity in one gulp," said Sam.

"Oh, no," Marcus said. "We have solved the mystery, but it doesn't have a happy ending."

"It's not solved yet," said Tommy. "Something is still not right."

Everybody looked at Tommy. Tommy tapped his foot on the floor. He was thinking. Sam and Marcus groaned. They wanted to leave. Tracker and Brutus were bored, too. They curled up on the floor and went to sleep. Only Tommy and Lucky paced around the room.

First Tommy looked in the cage. Then he looked at the cat. At last he knew what was wrong. "Cats don't swallow their food in one gulp," he said. "They take their time."

Jason snapped his fingers. "You're right," he said.

"Then where is Hoppity?" asked Sam.

Everyone looked up at the ceiling, searching for Hoppity. She was not in sight.

"*YIP, YIP, YIP,*" barked Lucky. He was not looking up at the ceiling. He was looking down and tugging at a big boot on the floor. He tipped it over. Out hopped Hoppity.

42

"Hurrah," said Jason. "You have solved the case of the flyaway parakeet. I think you are the best detective agency in the world."

"*YIP, YIP, ARF, ARF, BOW, WOW,*" barked Lucky, Tracker, and Brutus. All three of them knew that Jason was right.

The Secret
of the
Flashing Light

By Jane Swope

Dana didn't know what woke her up. She lay in her bed wide awake. The wind was blowing. A branch scratched across her screen.

She turned her eyes toward the window. The forsythia bush outside moved back and forth in the wind. Dana lay watching and listening, unable to get back to sleep.

Suddenly, she sat up. Had a ray of light flickered between the bare branches?

"Amy," she called to her sister who was sleeping in the twin bed next to hers. "Wake up."

Amy groaned and pushed herself deeper beneath the covers.

Dana glanced toward the window. It was dark. Then the light flicked on again.

"Amy," Dana called. Amy didn't move.

Dana got out of bed and walked cautiously to the window. With her heart pounding she looked out.

Her bedroom window looked out on Mrs. Greer's house. There were only a few feet of yard separating the two houses.

Dana waited for the light to reappear, feeling the cold of the winter night creep into her bare feet.

Finally, she saw it. It was weaker this time, but the beam lit the front of her nightgown.

"Amy, wake up," Dana said. She rushed to her sister's bed and shook her awake. "Amy, there's someone shining a flashlight out Mrs. Greer's bedroom window!"

Amy's eyes opened wide. "A burglar," she said. "I'll bet it's a burglar."

"You go to the window and watch," Dana said. "I'm going to wake Mom and Dad."

In a few minutes Dana returned. She pulled her dad over to the window. "Look, Dad. Someone is shining a light out Mrs. Greer's window."

"I haven't seen any light," Amy said. "I think she dreamed it."

"No, I didn't. I saw a light," Dana insisted.

Dana's dad stood watching the Greer house. "Well, I don't see anything, now," he said. "Let's go back to bed."

"Dad, call Mrs. Greer. Maybe there is a burglar in her house," Dana said.

"Honey, Mrs. Greer is a very old lady who needs her sleep. I'm not going to call her at this hour."

Dana stayed by the window after her dad and Amy had gone back to bed. *I know I saw a light,* she thought.

Determined to find an explanation, she reached for her jeans. "Amy, get dressed. We're going over to Mrs. Greer's to investigate."

Amy sighed but did as her older sister asked.

"There it is, again," Dana said. "It's very dim like the batteries are weak."

Amy ran to the window. "Where?" she asked.

"It's gone, but I saw it," Dana said. "Let's go."

Quietly, Dana and Amy closed the front door behind them. The winter wind whipped at their coats. They shivered. There was no moon and no sound but the wind whistling through the trees.

Amy stood close to Dana and whispered. "Let's go back inside, Dana."

Dana was tempted to run back into the warm, safe house, but she could not forget the light.

"No. Let's go look in that window." Dana took her sister's hand and led her around to the side of the house.

She stopped under Mrs. Greer's window. "Climb on my shoulders, Amy, and look inside."

Standing on Dana's shoulders, Amy pressed her nose to the screen outside Mrs. Greer's window.

"What do you see?" Dana asked.

"Nothing," Amy replied. "I don't see anything . . . Wait. I do see something. I see a dim light on the floor. It's flashing on and off."

"Let's go knock on the door," Dana said as she dropped Amy to the ground.

The girls ran to knock on Mrs. Greer's front door.

"Mrs. Greer, Mrs. Greer!" Dana called as she pounded on the door.

There was no answer.

"Let's go," Amy said. "We are going to get into a lot of trouble. What if Mom and Dad find out we are gone?"

"Hush," Dana said and knocked again.

The girls didn't realize a car had driven up to the curb in front of the house until a light flooded the porch.

"What is going on here?" a voice asked.

Dana caught her breath in surprise. Amy hid behind Dana.

A police car stood at the curb, its spotlight blinding the two of them.

"Something is definitely wrong in Mrs. Greer's house, officer," Dana said.

As the police officer came up the walk, lights filled the windows in Dana's house.

Dana and Amy trembled as the police officer walked toward them. Mom and Dad came out of the house and toward the girls.

Dana told her story. Amy agreed that there was a light in the bedroom.

"Mrs. Greer is an elderly lady," Dana's dad told the officer. "I didn't want to disturb her at this hour."

"Just go look in the window," Dana urged the officer, pulling at his uniform.

Returning to the front of the house, the officer reported what appeared to be a dim flashlight shining in the bedroom.

"Mrs. Greer keeps a key hidden behind a shutter," Dana's dad offered. "Maybe we should go in."

Inside, they found Mrs. Greer lying on the floor.

"Thank goodness you have come," she said. "I fell earlier. I think my hip is broken."

The officer went to call an ambulance.

Mrs. Greer continued. "I managed to reach the flashlight I keep on my bedside table. I kept shining the light at your house, hoping you would see it."

"Dana saw it," Amy said. "We didn't believe her at first, but she was sure something was wrong."

"Thank you, Dana," Mrs. Greer said as she was wheeled out to the ambulance. "You are a good neighbor."

The Mystery
of the
Missing Newspapers

By Ann Bixby Herold

When Ally added the house on Blueberry Lane to her newspaper route, she never thought there would be any kind of trouble. She'd ridden over after school on Friday to check the starting date. The house was hidden by trees at the end of a long driveway.

"Is Monday okay?" Mrs. Stout asked. "You'd better meet our new puppy and make friends if you're going to be stopping by every afternoon."

"Puppy?" Ally gasped when a big black mutt bounded out of the house.

Mrs. Stout laughed. "He has the sweetest nature. He licked the mail carrier's face this morning."

I bet the mail carrier was glad about that! Ally thought to herself.

"There's a new plastic tube nailed to a post down by the mailbox," Mrs. Stout said. "Leave the paper there. When do you collect the money?"

"Saturdays."

"Fine. Say good-bye to Ally, Blackie."

Blackie wriggled all over and barked.

On Monday afternoon, as Ally slipped the newspaper into the tube, Blackie galloped out of the bushes. There was no sign of Mrs. Stout.

"Are you allowed down here by yourself?" Ally asked him. "There are no neighbors and hardly any traffic, so I guess it's okay. I wish I had a dog. My mom won't let me have one because she works."

When she rode away, Blackie followed her. "Stay!" she called, and the dog stopped. "Go home, Blackie!"

He gave her a long, sad look and turned away.

On Tuesday, Blackie was there. And Wednesday. On Thursday Ally's friend, Mario, rode with her. Blackie seemed just as pleased to see Mario.

"He's smart," Ally said.

"Smart?" said Mario. "He's no good as a guard dog. He's not scary."

Ally glared at him. "His bark is scary, Mario. And he looks tough."

"Until he licks you," he laughed. "Some tough dog he is."

Ally didn't know anything was wrong until Saturday. Blackie greeted her as usual, and escorted her up the driveway.

A very different Mrs. Stout opened the door.

"You want me to pay you?" Her voice was cold.

Ally gulped. She'd heard about people who refused to pay, but she'd never met one before. "Here's today's paper and you owe me for five more," she said.

Mrs. Stout shook her head. "This is the first newspaper I've received from you, and this is the only one I'm paying for." She handed Ally fifty cents.

"But I *did* leave the papers," Ally protested.

"Then where are they?"

Blackie was sitting nearby, chewing on an old slipper. He looked up at Ally.

"Blackie?" Ally suggested desperately. The dog looked at her and burped.

Any other time, Ally would have laughed.

"If the paper isn't here Monday, I'm cancelling our order," Mrs. Stout said. "I have to go. I'm late for a meeting."

Ally rode to Mario's house.

"How can she say she didn't get them?" she asked in a worried voice. "Now I'll have to pay for all of them myself."

"Maybe somebody stole them," Mario suggested, trying to help.

"Who? Nobody else lives around there. What if Blackie took them? He could easily reach the tube."

"He's not that smart," said Mario.

"Yes he is. I bet the chewed leftovers are hidden in the bushes. Mrs. Stout's not home. Let's go and look for them."

They took turns acting as lookout. Blackie barked at them from a window. Mario and Ally searched all around the yard, even in the bushes. But nowhere did they find any chewed newspapers.

"You can't expect people to pay for something they didn't get," Ally's mother told her. "You'll just have to pay up."

Not yet, thought Ally.

On Monday Mario went with her again. According to plan they left the newspaper, patted Blackie, and rode away. Out of sight, they hid their bicycles and made their way back on foot.

Blackie already had the paper in his mouth by the time they got there.

"I told you!" Ally whispered as they watched him carry it away, his tail wagging.

Moments later, somewhere in the bushes, they heard chomping, ripping sounds.

By the time they found Blackie, the only sign of the newspaper was a ragged strip of the business section hanging from his mouth.

Ally snatched it away. "Bad dog!" she cried.

Blackie wagged his tail and burped.

"I know what happened to your newspapers," Ally told Mrs. Stout when she came home.

"Not now, please." She looked worried. "Blackie is due at the vet in ten minutes. There is something wrong with him. He hasn't eaten anything all week, and all he does is burp."

"Can eating a newspaper a day make a dog sick?" Ally held out the piece of newsprint. "This is all that's left of today's."

Blackie burped louder than ever.

"Blackie!" cried Mrs. Stout. "Get in the car!"

Later, Mrs. Stout told Ally, "The vet said Blackie had a bad case of indigestion. Wood pulp and ink aren't a good diet for a growing dog."

She paid for the missing newspapers. And she invited Alex and Mario over for ice cream.

Mr. Stout moved the tube. Ally had to stand on a box to reach it. Blackie still waited for her, so she always carried a dog biscuit in her pocket. Some days she stayed and played with him.

"He's smarter than he used to be," she told Mario. "Do you think eating all those words helped?"

"He'd need a twenty-volume set of encyclopedias," said Mario.

Alone on
Misery Island

By Barbee Oliver Carleton

The fog hung heavy over Misery Island. Jeff could see only to the end of the pier.

"There's a path that leads up to the house," said the lobsterman, handing up Jeff's suitcase. "Your Uncle Bill's at home, all right. That's his boat, the *Osprey*. Well, see you around, son."

"Thanks for the lift," called Jeff, as the engine burst into life and the lobster boat turned back noisily into the fog. Jeff stood for a moment as the sharp beat of the motor grew faint. He heard the clanging of the fog bell out on the Point.

Jeff picked up the heavy suitcase and started up the pier. Surprised, he paused beside the *Osprey.* That was odd. Her cockpit was completely bare. Her cabin door was padlocked, her cushions and deck chairs stored inside. Jeff was puzzled. "Why lock her up like this when he uses her every day?"

Jeff shrugged. Suddenly, he wanted to get out of the silent, watchful fog. He wanted to see Uncle Bill and hear his hearty, "Well, now, Jeff!"

Jeff struggled up the slippery path. His suitcase bumped his legs. Wet bayberry bushes brushed his face. The house should be right ahead now, up this steep path, and at the head of the cliff.

Uncle Bill would be surprised, all right. *With this fog,* thought Jeff, *he'll be glad I got a lift out here.* Then he frowned. "Funny he hasn't heard the boat and come to meet me, though," he muttered.

The rough path flattened, and there it was—a gray house, rising lonesomely out of the mist. Somehow the place looked deserted.

Jeff shivered but walked firmly to the front door and rapped heavily. He listened and heard only silence within.

"Uncle Bill!" he cried. "*UNCLE BILL!*" A sea gull screamed in the distance. Frantically, Jeff tried the door. It was locked. He called again, loudly. Nothing. There was no one else but Jeff on this lonely fog-bound island! He shook the door until he was out of breath.

Then he heard the sound of swiftly running footsteps behind him. Whirling about, he thought he saw a gray shadow move back into the spruces. "Uncle Bill?" he asked shakily. In answer he heard only the fog bell.

"Come on, Jeff," he told himself scornfully. "Grow up!" But his hands were icy. "Maybe there's a back door," Jeff gasped. He must get inside.

He was scrambling over a slippery place when he heard the sound of running feet again. Jeff turned sharply, lost his balance, and rolled down the steep rock. He struck out wildly with hands and knees. A bush tore at his arm and he snatched at it. It held. Spread-eagled, he clung to the face of the cliff. Below plunged the grayness of space. Whether sand or sea, or how far below, he could not tell. He listened. Only the faint shushing of the tide reached his ears. He could be ten feet up, or one hundred!

Jeff figured his chances. Something had happened to Uncle Bill, maybe something awful. And Jeff was the only one on the whole island. Yet he *had* heard footsteps, and he *had* seen that shape!

Jeff tried to shift his weight. How long could he last here? His hands, already cold, soon became numb. "Unless you get moving," he told himself grimly, "it's down, and fast."

It took courage to let go of that bush, even with one hand. Cautiously, he felt along the ledge above. There was a tiny crack, wide enough for his fingers. He groped with one foot for a higher toehold. Slowly, blindly, Jeff worked his way upward. Below waited space, fog-filled and secret. Who knew what waited above? Stealthily, so as not to give away his position, he climbed until the high edge of the rock showed dark against the sky. Then, with a groan, he was up and over.

A tall shape was bearing down on him. A long arm whipped around him. "Well, now, Jeff!" boomed a familiar voice. And Jeff, gasping, looked up at Uncle Bill.

Jeff grinned weakly. "Surprise!"

Uncle Bill laughed and shook his head. "Uh, uh. You left your suitcase at the front door. And then I heard you puffing like a porpoise over the cliff. If you want to explore, why not take the path? It's easier."

"What path?" asked Jeff as they started back to the house.

"The path that leads down to the beach. Fifty feet down," he added dryly.

"I slipped and fell over."

"Well I'll be," said Uncle Bill.

They went into the cozy living room. As Uncle Bill lit the fire and started work on a sizeable snack, Jeff brought him up to date.

"And then I caught a ride out with Mr. Wilkes, and you weren't here. I heard someone following me, and I ran around the house, and—you know the rest."

Uncle Bill nodded. "You had a rough few minutes. You heard the foxes, Jeff—shy little things. They're active creatures, all right, but harmless."

"I wish I found that out sooner," said Jeff weakly.

Uncle Bill slapped hamburgers onto the griddle. "I heard you coming in around the Point. I was just rowing alongshore and yelled, but I couldn't make you hear me. I needed a tow."

Jeff looked up from his task of whipping cream for the hot chocolate. "A tow? But the *Osprey* is tied up at the float. That's what made me worried about you."

Uncle Bill looked wise. "That's *my* surprise. Jeff, we now have a sailboat—a little beauty—and finished just in time for your visit."

"WOW!" said Jeff.

"I've been teaching myself the ropes. Haven't used the *Osprey* for a week. So I went out for my sail this morning and ran her aground."

"Landlubber," teased Jeff.

"Give us time," laughed his uncle. "Well, I had to wait for the tide to lift her off. By then the wind had gone down and the fog had come in. I had to row home."

"Tsk, tsk," Jeff said as he munched peacefully on his hamburger. "And I thought I was in a jam."

The Gold Cat Lady Mystery

By Colleen Archer

Although David, Susan, and Darren Bradford anticipated adventure on their horseback holiday in the Rocky Mountains, nothing could have prepared them for "Sinister Sam" and the gold cat lady.

"I think Mom and Dad are at the front of the line," said twelve-year-old Susan to her brothers. As she spoke, she glared at the hunched back of Sam Jaffe directly ahead. Sam was a big, middle-aged man with a nasty disposition, and it was eight-year-old Darren who had nicknamed him

"Sinister." Each time Darren caught his sister's eye, he would point to Sam and hiss quietly through his teeth like a snake.

The children's instinctive dislike of Sam was balanced by their attraction to a second lone traveller, the gold cat lady. They called her this because of a solid gold cat pin she wore on her lapel and a golden haired cat she carried in a knapsack on her back. Though her hair was white, she rode elegantly and effortlessly, and her rose-tinted glasses and cream-colored outfit stood out among the grubby sweat shirts and jeans of the other riders.

When the riders discovered a clearing for their first rest stop of the day, David, Susan, and Darren dismounted and headed straight for their new friend, Janet Carter. Her silky cat, Gem, was already stretching his legs, his blue eyes reflecting the bright July sun.

"Look at his feet," whispered Darren. "He looks like he stepped in a can of white paint."

"*Shh—,*" warned Susan, tossing her long yellow braid, but Mrs. Carter only laughed.

"He's a Birman, Darren," she explained, "and all Birmans have dark paws with white gloves. They're very rare, and some people say that they're descended from sacred cats."

As if on cue, Gem yawned aristocratically while Darren and Susan laughed with delight. They didn't notice that their dark-haired fourteen-year-old brother wasn't laughing. David was watching Sam Jaffe, and he didn't like what he saw.

Sam had left his horse and gone with a group of naturalists, supposedly to photograph wildlife. A moment later he vanished and then reappeared on top of a hill. He had a long lens on his camera, a telephoto lens, but the lens wasn't aimed at a mule deer or a bighorn sheep. Instead it was aimed right at Janet Carter!

That night, as the children were playing cards in their tent, David told them what he had seen.

"We've all got to keep an eye on Sam," he ordered his brother and sister. "He's up to something, but I don't know what."

The children watched Sam for three days but still couldn't decide what he was doing. He would disappear at each rest stop, but the kids always lost sight of him once he entered the trees. Then on the last day of the trip the mystery was solved.

"How about a shampoo before breakfast?" Mrs. Carter asked Susan, removing her large sunglasses and revealing for the first time her strikingly beautiful face. Mrs. Carter and Susan filled basins with dipper after dipper of water from the big tubs heating on the fire while Gem rolled playfully at their feet. They had just started lathering when Gem arched his back suddenly and hissed.

"Marlene!"

Mrs. Carter looked around and Sam's camera clicked, then clicked again.

"Beautiful. Thanks!" And Sam Jaffe was gone.

Mrs. Carter's face was white—*whiter than it should have just been just because someone took her picture,* thought Susan—but her voice was calm.

"Can you and your brothers come to my tent in ten minutes? I have a secret I'd like to share with just the three of you."

"So that's my story," she concluded a half-hour later as the children sat wide-eyed on the tent floor in front of her. "Since I retired from the movies twenty years ago, the press hasn't stopped pestering me. They wrote terrible things about me when I was young, and now that I'm old I just want to be left alone."

"You mean all Sam Jaffe wants is photographs?" asked David.

"Sam Jaffe wants money, and a national story on Marlene Mitchell could make him a small fortune. A man like that would write any lies to go with his pictures. Still, I don't see what I can do about it now."

It was a sad and silent ride for the children that afternoon. In another hour they would be back at the corral and Sam would sell his story. They were passing by a deep mountain stream when suddenly David had an idea. He motioned to Susan and Darren. They whispered together, then . . .

"Yahoo!" David charged behind Sam's buckskin mare while Susan and Darren came alongside, screeching and waving their hats. Sam was caught completely off guard as his spooked mare leaped sideways into the water to escape her crazy pursuers. Sam fell off and floundered noisily, turning just in time to see his loaded camera come loose from the saddle horn and drift slowly downstream.

Back home, David, Susan, and Darren were grounded for a full week by their angry parents, who simply couldn't understand what had possessed their normally well-behaved children to act in such a manner.

"I also can't figure out why that rich Mrs. Carter insisted on paying for Sam Jaffe's camera," said Mr. Bradford to his wife. "It should have come out of the kids' allowances. And as for giving them her gold pin . . ."

"I think," said Mrs. Bradford as she slowly filled the kettle for tea, "that there was far more to the story than anybody told us. It's funny, but that

Janet Carter reminded me of someone else. If only I could think who!"

Meanwhile in the family room, David, Susan, and Darren were eating popcorn and watching an early 1950s Marlene Mitchell movie on TV. Susan was wearing a solid gold cat pin on her sweater, and every few minutes she and her brothers would look from the pin to the lovely face on the television screen, and all three of them would smile mysteriously.

The Tiger Hunt

By Sally Walker

"I'm going on a Tiger hunt when I get home from school," Marybeth told her teacher at preschool.

"How exciting! Just like the bear hunts we do at story time?" Mrs. Manning asked.

"My Tiger hunt is not pretend," said Marybeth.

"I see," said Mrs. Manning. "Will you be travelling in an airplane for your hunt?"

Marybeth giggled and shook her head. "No, I won't need one for my Tiger hunt."

On the way home Marybeth skipped ahead of her father. At the corner she smiled at the crossing guard. "I'm going on a Tiger hunt when I get home from school."

"You had better bring a net. Tigers can be pretty wild," said the crossing guard.

Marybeth laughed and shook her head. "I won't need one on my Tiger hunt." She waved good-bye after she and her father crossed the street.

At home Marybeth helped her father make lunch. She spread peanut butter on two slices of bread while he sliced an apple. They each poured a glass of milk.

"I'm going on a Tiger hunt as soon as I finish my lunch." Marybeth crunched a slice of apple between her teeth.

"Need any help?" her father asked.

Marybeth thought for a minute. "No, not today. I'll go myself. But I think I'll bring my flashlight. Sometimes it's dark on a Tiger hunt."

"Good idea," said her father.

Marybeth carried her plate to the sink, and then ran to her room. Deep inside her toy box she could see just the end of her blue flashlight sticking out from beneath a stuffed bear. She dug in and pulled it out. She pushed the switch with her thumb and a bright circle of light appeared on the ceiling.

Marybeth looked around her room. There was no Tiger in there.

She crossed the hall and peeked into her parents' room. The closet door was slightly open. Pushing her way through the jungle of pant legs, Marybeth shined her light into the back corners.

"Tiger, are you here?" she whispered. No answer. No Tiger. The hunt must go on.

Marybeth turned on the basement light. She tiptoed down the steps, flashing her light from side to side. She could feel her heart beating. Even with the overhead light on, she still didn't like going to the basement. Spiderwebs hung from the ceiling, and the corners were dark. Marybeth heard water gurgling inside the pipes as her father washed the lunch dishes in the kitchen sink. She glanced behind the clothes dryer and on top of the bookshelf.

"Tiger, are you here?" she whispered. No answer. No Tiger. The hunt must go on.

Marybeth hurried back up the stairs. She closed the door tightly behind her and sighed with relief. Marybeth went into the living room. She crawled into the long dark cave behind the couch.

"Tiger, are you here?" she whispered. Two yellow eyes opened near the back of the cave. They gleamed in the dim light. Slowly, Marybeth began to crawl backward out from behind the couch cave. The yellow eyes came after her. A low rumbling echoed inside the cave. Marybeth waited.

Soon an orange-striped head poked out from behind the couch. "*R-r-r-a-o-w?*"

Marybeth burst out laughing. "Tiger, you silly cat. You have dust hanging on your whiskers." Marybeth wiped it away and scratched behind Tiger's ears. "I missed you while I was at school."

Tiger purred loudly and rubbed his head against her leg. Marybeth's Tiger hunt was over.

The Case of the
Missing Redhead

By Elaine Pageler

My partner, Murph, and I had worked hard to convert my tree house into a detective agency. We had even dangled a bell over the side for callers, but no one ever rang it. So when it jangled one day, we jumped sky high.

There stood a little girl with a tear-stained face and a piggy bank under her arm. "I'm Becky," she called. "I need a de-tect-ive. Someone is missing."

We made a flying leap for the ground. "Mitchell and McMurphy at your service," Murph announced. "Finding missing persons is our specialty."

"My Sally Doll is gone," began Becky.

"Doll!" I snorted.

"Cool it," whispered Murph, punching me in the ribs and pointing to the piggy bank.

"I took Sally Doll for a ride in her buggy," continued Becky. "She likes to get rides. But then Mommy called me for lunch. And when I came back, Sally Doll was gone."

"Show us the scene of the crime," ordered Murph.

She led us down the alley to her house. There in the backyard stood the baby buggy.

Becky's face clouded up and she sobbed, "Sally Doll is the prettiest one in the whole world. She has red hair and a blue dress."

"Stop crying! We'll find her," said Murph, searching the buggy. "Hey! Look at this!" He pulled out a rubber dog bone.

"Rats!" I exclaimed. Rats is a big, shaggy dog who belongs to the Donderfields. He is notorious for his pack-rat habits. Whenever he steals, the dog leaves something else behind.

"We'll solve the case of the missing redhead and return her to you for a reward, of course," said Murph, giving me a wink.

The three of us hurried to Mrs. Donderfield's house. She was out in her yard cutting roses. Rats sat nearby chewing on someone's football.

"Hi," I called. "Did your dog bring home a red-haired doll with a blue dress?"

Mrs. Donderfield put down her scissors and stared at us. "So that's how that doll got here. I had put two boxes of old clothes out in the front yard for the church bazaar. When the truck arrived, we found the doll lying nearby. Guessing that someone had meant to donate it, I put it into one of the boxes."

"Is that the church bazaar that's happening on Ninth Street?" Murph asked.

When she nodded, Murph, Becky, and I raced down the street. Five blocks later, we skidded to a stop. The parking lot behind the church was a beehive of activity. There were tables piled high with junk, but no doll.

"Have you seen a red-haired doll with a blue dress?" I asked one woman.

"Ruth," she yelled. "You remember what happened to that doll?"

A women three tables away shouted, "I gave it to Mrs. Crisp's baby to keep her quiet. They went home a while ago."

"My Sally Doll," sobbed Becky.

"Hold it, kid," said Murph. "You've employed two detectives who just happen to know Mrs. Crisp and her baby. Come on!"

Mrs. Crisp was in the kitchen. Her baby still sat in the stroller. Instead of a doll, she had a bottle in her hands.

"I have no idea what happened to the doll," confessed Mrs. Crisp. "I don't remember seeing it when we got home."

The baby threw her bottle across the floor.

"She does that all the time," complained Mrs. Crisp, cleaning up the mess.

Murphy led us outside. "It's obvious that the kid threw the doll away on their walk home. That sidewalk goes past the park. Sally Doll must be in those bushes."

Unfortunately, the park was two blocks long. "That's a lot of bushes," I griped. "Too bad that doll can't talk."

"She can," said Becky. "Sally Doll says 'Mama'."

Murph shot me a glance, shook his head, and started searching. Two hours later, we had piles of bottles and cans, but no doll.

"Thanks, kids," said the caretaker, walking over to them. "I've been meaning to clean that area."

"We're hunting for a red-haired doll with a blue dress," I told him.

"Oh, that. I gave it to her," he said, pointing to a woman sitting on a bench.

Becky's eyes lit up. "Grandma!" she cried.

"Hi, honey," called the woman. "I was just on my way to your house. Look what Grandma has for you." She held up the red-haired doll with the blue dress.

We watched as they walked away. Becky was clutching Sally Doll in one hand and her piggy bank in the other.

"There goes our reward," I muttered.

"At least we can sell these at the recycling center," said Murphy, gathering up the bottles and cans.

Later, we were back in the tree house when the bell rang. There stood Becky. "I forgot to give you the reward," she called.

We scrambled down the ladder and held out our hands, expecting the piggy bank.

Becky gave us a sweet smile and said, "You're good de-tect-ives. Here is your reward, Sally Doll's older sister, Annie Doll." With that, she plopped a one-armed, baldheaded, ragged doll into our hands and ran off.

And that was the end of the case of the missing redhead.

Mr. Masters's Mystery

By Jane K. Priewe

Jenny nudged Pam. "What's Mr. Masters planting this time? He always has the prettiest flowers."

"Let's find out." Pam jumped from the porch, startling a blue jay searching for insects under a bush. She laughed when he squawked.

The girls ran down the sidewalk and flopped on the thick grass near where their gray-haired friend cultivated a large, round flower bed.

"Morning, ladies. What are you up to this summer vacation?"

"Nothing much," Pam said.

"What're those, Mr. Masters?" Jenny pointed to three sturdy-looking plants, each about a foot high. "Are they weeds?"

Mr. Masters chuckled. "I don't think so, Jenny, but I didn't plant them. I didn't see who planted them, but I'm going to let them grow. Someone must have sowed those seeds for a reason." Mr. Masters winked at the girls. "There's a mystery for you to solve this summer."

"Yeah!" Jenny exclaimed. "We'll be detectives, Pam, and solve Mr. Masters's Mystery."

"How?"

"Keep your eyes open, girls, and you'll discover what the plants are, who planted them, and why. If you answer all three questions before school starts, I'll treat you to ice-cream cones."

"A cinch!" Jenny said, but three weeks later their mystery was still unsolved.

"You suppose he was teasing us?" Pam asked as they examined the plants that now towered over colorful pansies and zinnias in the flower bed. "Mr. Masters said they weren't weeds, but I never saw anything grow faster, did you?"

Jenny shook her head. "Maybe they're magic vines like in 'Jack and the Beanstalk'."

Pam snickered. "That's a fairy tale! Look, Jen! Is that a flower coming?"

Jenny stood on tiptoes and gently bent one of the tall plants to see its top. "Could be. What goofy-looking plants!"

The blossoms grew larger and stretched out wider while the mysterious plants stretched toward the sky. In another week, they were so tall they dwarfed the girls. Nobody bothered the flower bed except birds and occasionally some neighborhood cats and dogs.

One morning Jenny raced to Pam's house. "I know what they are!" She hopped around in excitement. "I saw one in a flower book. They're sunflowers, Pam!"

"Sunflowers!" Pam echoed. "Now, who planted them, and why?"

Jenny traded her happy smile for a look of determination. "We'll find out. See if we don't!"

The huge sunflowers opened. They stood like three round-faced, giant guards over the pansies and zinnias.

One day Jenny saw a squirrel skitter into the flower bed. He sat among the zinnias near a tall sunflower and nibbled on something he picked off the ground. After a noisy blue jay chased him into Mr. Masters's maple tree, Jenny carefully picked her way to the sunflower. On the ground she saw dried seed shells.

"The little squirrel was eating seeds that fell off the sunflower," she told Pam later that day. "Someone must have planted those sunflowers for their seeds.

"Even people eat sunflower seeds, Jen," Pam said. "So who planted them?"

Jenny grinned. "A neighbor? Someone who wanted to play a joke on Mr. Masters?"

"Let's ask around the neighborhood," Pam suggested. "We'll tell people about the mystery and maybe someone'll confess."

The girls questioned people up and down the entire street, but nobody admitted to being the seed planter.

"We know they're sunflowers, and we think they were planted so someone could eat the seeds," Jenny told Mr. Masters next morning.

"But we can't figure out who did the planting," Pam said, depressed.

"There's still a week until school opens." The old gentleman pointed to the sunflowers rustling in a gentle breeze. "They're dry now. The planter should be busy. Keep watching."

The next day Jenny looked up from the Monopoly game she and Pam were playing on her porch. One of the sunflowers was bent toward the ground from the weight of something blue clinging to its dry blossom.

"Look, Pam. A blue jay on a sunflower."

The jay flew to Mrs. Henry's yard. It strutted to where Mrs. Henry had been staking chrysanthemums beside her house. The bird pecked at the ground, then flew back to the sunflower. It made four trips between the sunflower and Mrs. Henry's yard while the girls watched.

They ran to where the blue jay had been pecking in the dirt. Jenny stooped, and carefully dug up a sunflower seed.

"We've solved the mystery, Pam! Who'd have thought a bird could be that smart!"

Later, in the ice-cream parlor, the girls laughed when Mr. Masters told them that they could order triple-decker cones.

"Single scoops'll be fine," Pam said. "We're giving you our going-out-of-the-detective-business special rate."

"But we would like some of those sunflower seeds, Mr. Masters." Jenny licked her pink bubble gum ice cream. "We're going to plant them in our backyards for the blue jays."

"I'll have a triple cone to celebrate that good news!" Mr. Masters said. "If you'll grow them, I can have a neat flower bed in my front yard again. Those sunflowers looked terrible!"

Jenny giggled. "The blue jays didn't think so."

THE ZOO DETECTIVE

By Ellen Javernick

"Don't look now," said Sammy. "But I think someone's following us."

"No way," said B.J.

"She was beside us over near the lions, she was near us in the petting zoo, and now she's here in the monkey house."

"You shouldn't pay so much attention to everybody else. Besides, if someone's looking at you, it's probably because you are acting like a monkey."

Sammy glared at his sister. Just because she was seven didn't mean she knew everything. He moved a little so he could see the lady's reflection in the glass on the front of the orangutans' cage. She looked almost old enough to be a mother. She was wearing a pink shirt and sandals.

B.J. interrupted Sammy's thinking. "Sammy, take a look at the orangutans. Don't you think they ought to wear diapers?"

Sammy giggled. Their pink bottoms did look sort of naked.

They were both still giggling when Mother pushed Jody's stroller up beside them.

"May we go to Bird World next?" begged B.J.

"Jody and I just caught up to you."

"George, George," said Jody clapping her hands and pointing to one of the monkeys.

"Jody thinks that monkey's Curious George," said Sammy.

Mother smiled. "We will stay and watch 'George' for a few minutes. You two may start over to Bird World, but, B.J., watch Sammy carefully."

The children ran down the path to see the penguins. Sammy was sure that B.J. was not the only one watching him. The lady he'd seen before seemed to be staring straight at him. Sammy pulled on B.J.'s sleeve. "She's still following us."

"You are silly, Sammy. There's no law that says other people can't go the same way we go. Stop looking at people. Look at the penguins."

Sammy looked. He saw a man in a zoo uniform tossing fish to the penguins.

When the zoo keeper's fish buckets were empty, Mother still wasn't there. "Let's start inside," suggested Sammy.

Sammy and B.J. saw a little beach and some sandpipers. They saw a toucan on a branch. Then they went into a room filled with plants. Birds were flying everywhere. A hummingbird flew straight at B.J.

"It is because you have a red shirt on," explained a zoo keeper.

"Let's go tell mother about your shirt and the hummingbird," said B.J.

Sammy and B.J. went back past the toucan and the sandpiper. Then Sammy saw the lady. She had followed them back out of Bird World.

"B.J., I'm telling you, she's following us! We've got to lose her!"

Sammy wriggled away from B.J. and ran down one of the paths. B.J. tore after him, but after a while, Samy was nowhere to be seen. There were bushes all up and down the path, and Sammy could be hiding in any of them!

Just then Mother and Jody spotted B.J., who was searching around frantically. "Honey, what's wrong? Where's Sammy?"

B.J. didn't know what to say. Then she saw the lady that Sammy was talking about headed toward them. Maybe Sammy was right!

B.J. started to tell Mother the whole story, but Sammy came out of one of the bushes and interrupted. "See that lady. She is following us."

Just then the lady walked over to Sammy's mother. I am sorry if I scared your son." She showed Sammy and Mother a zoo worker's badge. "You would make a good detective," she said to Sammy. "You are the first person to catch me, and I have been following folks all summer."

"Why do you follow people?" asked Sammy.

"It is my summer job. I am doing research. The zoo director wants to learn about the people who visit the zoo. He wants to know if they read our signs and follow our paths. He wants to know how long they stay at each exhibit. He wants to know what they think about the facilities. See what I wrote down about your family."

Sammy looked at the map the lady was holding. There was a red line showing where Sammy and B.J. had walked. "You were hard to follow," said the lady. "I hope my next folks are easier."

"Can't you follow us anymore?" asked Sammy.

"That would be fun, but since you caught me, I must find another family to follow. I hope you enjoy the rest of your stay at our zoo."

"We will," said Sammy. "And we won't give away your secret."

The Talking Cat

By L. H. Phinney

Most folks were afraid of Old Pete, the lame tailor. But he was the only tailor in town, so people had to go to him.

He wouldn't speak to anyone very often. He would only grunt out the price of a repaired jacket or shirt. He lived alone except for a big yellow cat, and people didn't like the cat any better than they liked Old Pete. A few people claimed they had heard the cat talk. Some people said Pete was a miser, and others said that he was some sort of witch. But nobody talked to him enough to find out.

Jed Horton had seen him limping along the street and thought he looked like a storybook pirate, with his long gray hair and tangled gray whiskers. Jed and his mother had only recently moved into the little cottage next to Old Pete's shop. Jed was ten years old and was just getting acquainted in his new school. He knew Old Pete only by sight, but he was soon to know him better.

It was a December morning—cold, stormy, icy. Jed saw Old Pete limping slowly along with his cane. Just as Pete reached his shop door, he slipped and fell heavily. For a moment he lay quietly. Then, getting on his hands and knees, he crawled into the shop and shut the door.

Nothing more was seen of Old Pete that day. A few customers came to his shop door and found it locked. Jed had told his mother of Old Pete's fall, and when Jed came from school she suggested that he go over and see if Pete was badly hurt. Jed didn't like the errand very well, but he went.

He ran across the little yard and rapped on the door of the shop. There was no answer. Jed rapped again—and again. Then a hoarse voice called, "Who's there?"

"Me, Jed Horton. I live next door. Mother wants to know if you got hurt badly when you fell. Can I run any errands for you?"

Jed heard a mutter inside the shop, then a shout, then more muttering. "Hey kid! Clear out! Oh! Ouch! Wait, you nosy kid. Can you build a fire?"

"Yes, sir," Jed said. "I've built ours."

"Build mine. Wait, I'll open the door. Oh, ow, I'm lame!"

Jed heard a shuffling in the shop, then the door opened. Old Pete could hardly stand upright. He sank into a ragged old armchair. There was no other furniture except a tiny end table and a sewing machine. A small stove was in one corner, a sink in another. A door opened into a small bedroom, and another into a shed.

"Wood in shed. Paper by stove. Here's match." Old Pete groaned.

On the back of Pete's chair sat the big yellow cat. As Jed took the match from Pete's fingers, the cat spoke in a shrill, high voice. "Hurry up," he said. "I'm cold."

Jed dropped the match. He nearly turned and ran.

"What's wrong?" Old Pete growled. "You scared of the cat?"

Jed picked up the match and, keeping an eye on the cat, soon had a fire burning in the little stove.

"Can I get you something to eat?" he asked.

"Bread and milk," Pete said. "Store down street. Dishes in sink. Here's money."

Jed took the money and ran to the store, stopping only to tell his mother a little about Old Pete. He didn't mention the talking cat. It didn't seem it could be true.

Jed came back and washed the dishes in the sink. He set out the bread and milk on the little stand. Then he gave the cat some milk in a dish by the stove.

The cat lapped it up, then distinctly said, "More!"

Old Pete ignored the cat. "Pile wood by stove," he said. "I'm lame. Come tomorrow. Here." He handed Jed fifty cents.

Jed tried to refuse the money but Old Pete shouted, "Take what you get and get out!"

The cat said, "Good night. Come again."

At home, Jed told his mother about the cat.

"I wonder . . ." she said thoughtfully. "Well, see what happens tomorrow."

In the morning, Mrs. Horton sent over a breakfast of oatmeal, toast, and coffee. Old Pete scowled as Jed set it out on the stand.

"How much?" he growled.

"Nothing," Jed replied. "We hope you feel better."

The cat came over, smelled the oatmeal, and said, "Hot! I want milk."

Pete gave Jed money and a milk bottle without a word. Jed bought some milk and fed the cat.

Pete gave Jed one dollar when he went home. That night Mrs. Horton sent over a plate of beef stew. The cat ate some of that and said, "Very good."

Old Pete seemed to be better. He could walk around without much pain.

"All right tomorrow," he said gruffly. "Don't come. I like living alone—with a cat that talks." Then he laughed and looked almost pleasant. "Now, don't tell anyone this, boy," he said. "I'm a ventriloquist. Throw my voice. Make anything seem to talk. Was with shows for years. Then got lame and had to quit. But keep it a secret, will you? Most fun I have these days is mystifying people."

He handed Jed five dollars. "Take it," he said. "Worth it. Tell your ma. Get out now! Good-bye."

The cat seemed to call "good-bye" too, as Jed went out the door.

"I thought that must be how the cat was made to seem to talk," Mrs. Horton said, when Jed got home. "Old Pete is a strange old fellow, but you and I will never be afraid of him again. And we'll keep his secret as long as he wants us to."